This Book Belongs To:

_____

sleeping Beauty

Illustrated by Pam Storey
Story re-told by Grace De La Touche

© 1996, Landoll, Inc.
Ashland, Ohio 44805
© 1992, Grandreams Limited

A long time ago and far away there lived a King and a Queen. They were very happy, for their first child, a girl, had been born.

"We must have a grand christening for her," said the King, who was delighted to have a daughter.

"We must invite all the fairies of the kingdom to bless her," said the Queen.

"How many are there now?" asked the King.

"Twelve or thirteen," said his wife. "Send the invitations. We'll soon find out."

There were twelve fairies, and they were all sent invitations. A thirteenth fairy had not been heard of for so long that it was presumed that she was dead. No invitation was sent.

The day of the christening was sunny and bright. The Princess was named Briar Rose, and the fairies began to give their gifts.

"She shall be beautiful," said the first.

"She shall be wise," said the second.

"She shall be good," said the third.

"She shall be kind," said the fourth.

The gifts continued in this way, wishing all that was good for Briar Rose. Eleven of the twelve fairies had given their gifts when the room suddenly went dark. After a great flash of light a small dark figure stood in front of the King and Queen.

It was the thirteenth fairy.

"Why wasn't I invited to the christening?" she screamed.

She was furious at being left out.

"All the fairies of the kingdom have given their blessings. Well, here's mine for the Princess. On her sixteenth birthday she will prick her finger on a spinning wheel and die."

Another flash of light and the fairy was gone.

"But we thought she was dead," said the King. "What can we do?"

The Queen was in tears.

The twelfth fairy stepped forward.

"There is still my gift for Briar Rose," she said. "The fairy's curse cannot be undone, but I can change it a little. She will prick her finger, but instead of dying she will fall into a deep sleep that will last one hundred years."

There was a great hubbub in the hall as everyone discussed the events.

The following day the King issued a proclamation, ordering that all spinning wheels

and spindles were to be destroyed. Throughout
the land there were great fires as the spinning
wheels were burned.

Over the years, the Princess grew into a
lovely girl. All who met her were enchanted by
her.

Eventually, the bad fairy's wish was
forgotten. All spinning wheels and spindles had
been destroyed, so there was no reminder. And
the fairy was not heard of again.

And so, on Briar Rose's sixteenth birthday, the King and Queen were due to arrive back from a far away visit. There was to be a large birthday party for the Princess.

Briar Rose was wandering around the palace. Everyone was preparing for the party, so she could please herself where she went. As there were still parts of the palace that she had never set foot in, she decided to go exploring.

"I wonder what is in the Great South Tower," she said. All the servants and courtiers wished her a happy birthday as she made her way across the palace.

That part of the palace was very old, and there were very few people there. The base of the tower was in a corridor. The entrance was a small, very solid looking door. The key was on the outside.

"It's very stiff," said the Princess, as she turned the key. "There! It's open!"

Stairs led up the tower in front of her. She began to climb them.

Meanwhile, her parents had arrived back at the palace.

"Has anyone seen the Princess?" asked the King.

"Today is her sixteenth birthday - the day when the curse may fall. Somebody must know where she is."

Nearly everyone had seen her, but nobody knew where she had been going.

"She must be found," said the Queen. "If the prophecy is to come true, today is the day."

A search of the palace and the grounds began.

Meanwhile, the Princess had reached the top of the tower where there was another door. This time there was no key and the door was slightly open.

"There must be a wonderful view of the rest of the palace and grounds from the window," said the Princess. Then she heard a strange whirring sound. It was unlike anything that she had ever heard before.

She pushed the door open and went into the room. There, in the middle, sat an old woman working at a spinning wheel. Behind her was an enormous bed.

The wheel was making the noise.

"What are you doing?" asked Briar Rose. "I have never seen one of those before, what is it?"

"It is a spinning wheel," said the old woman. "Would you like to try it my dear?"

"Oh, may I?" asked Briar Rose.

She sat on the stool in front of the wheel and the wheel whirred round. As soon as she touched the spindle she pricked her finger. She fell to the floor in a deep sleep. The old woman, who was really the thirteenth fairy in disguise, picked her up and laid her on the bed.

At that moment, all over the palace, people began to fall asleep. The cooks who were preparing for the party fell asleep over the stirring and tasting. The scullery maids fell asleep over the washing up. The laundry maid fell asleep over her washing. The chamber maids fell asleep while they dusted, polished and prepared for the party.

The King and Queen, the courtiers and the guests fell asleep in the Great Hall. The guards fell asleep at their posts. The search parties looking for the Princess fell asleep while they searched - in the gardens, in the corridors, in the spare rooms, and some in the oldest part of the palace.

Even the flies fell asleep on the stable walls. The birds and the butterflies fell asleep in the palace gardens. So did the wild rabbits that raided the palace vegetable gardens. The gardeners and their helpers, who were busy chasing off the rabbits, fell asleep in mid-chase.

In the hearths the fires died down and the meat stopped cooking. The kitchen maid stopped plucking the chicken.

The entire palace fell asleep, along with the Princess.

A hedge of briar roses sprang up around the palace, protecting it from the outside world.

Years passed, and from time to time a King's son would come to the famous briar hedge to try and find the mysterious sleeping Princess that the legend spoke of. But none got through. The hedge was too strong and the Princes were cut to bits.

A hundred years passed and the tale of the Sleeping Beauty, as the Princess was known, became a great legend. Very few people believed she existed.

One day a King's son came to the nearby village.

"Legend says," an old man was speaking in the village square. "Legend says that the Princess lies asleep behind that great briar hedge just outside the village. In my grandfather's day, you could see the topmost turret of her tower, so they say."

The Prince stopped to listen. "Where can I find this hedge?" he asked.

"Just beyond the village, young sir," said the old man. "If you're going to try, you'll need more luck than the other young men who have had a go."

"I shall try," said the Prince. "We have heard of Sleeping Beauty in my kingdom."

The Prince went to the hedge and held up his sword. He went to strike at the hedge, but where his sword met the thorns, great roses bloomed instead. A path opened for him, for the one hundred years were up. The curse was lifting.

The hedge seemed to disappear before him.

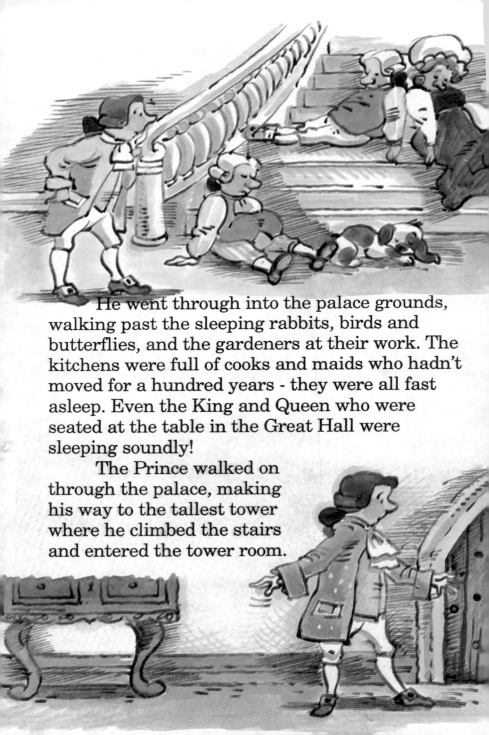

He went through into the palace grounds, walking past the sleeping rabbits, birds and butterflies, and the gardeners at their work. The kitchens were full of cooks and maids who hadn't moved for a hundred years - they were all fast asleep. Even the King and Queen who were seated at the table in the Great Hall were sleeping soundly!

The Prince walked on through the palace, making his way to the tallest tower where he climbed the stairs and entered the tower room.

There on the bed he saw Briar Rose fast asleep.

"She is so lovely," he said. He had fallen completely in love with her. "How can I wake her?"

He leant over and gently kissed her.

Briar Rose's eyelids flickered and she woke up. The first person she saw was the Prince and she fell in love with him.

Together they walked down to the Great
Hall. The King and Queen were just waking up,
when the Prince and Briar Rose entered.

The cooks in the kitchen woke up to carry
on preparing the food and the chambermaids
carried on with their work.

The party was still to be held, but it was

an engagement party instead of a birthday
party. The Prince and Briar Rose were to be
married.

  The hedge disappeared and the village
saw the palace again and realized the legend
had been true.

  The bad fairy was never heard of again.